TALES OF TERROR'S
ANTHOLOGIES OF TERROR
2016

Author: **Steve Hutchison**
Publisher: **Shade Art & Code**

Copyright © 2016 **Tales of Terror**
All rights reserved

WWW.**TERROR**.CA

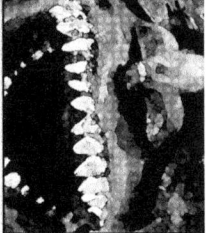

Copyright © 2016 by **Steve Hutchison**
All rights reserved. This book or any portion thereof may not be reproduced or used in any manner whatsoever without the express written permission of the publisher except for the use of brief quotations in a book review or scholarly journal.

This is the printed version of an online promotional tool. The images and screen captures were altered. They are used for marketing purposes; for authors, filmmakers and distributors.

First Printing: 2016
ISBN-13: 978-1541037595
ISBN-10: 1541037596

Design, reviews, ratings, analysis and gamification: Steve Hutchison - steve@shade.ca

Bookstores and wholesalers: Please contact books@terror.ca.

Tales of Terror
tales@terror.ca
www.terror.ca

INTRODUCTION

THIS BOOK CONTAINS 54 HORROR ANTHOLOGY FILM REVIEWS.

THE MOVIES ARE SORTED FROM BEST TO WORST. THE RANKING OF EACH FILM IS ESTABLISHED BY THE SUM OF 7 TYPES OF RATINGS: STARS, GIMMICK, REWATCHABILITY, STORY, CREATIVITY, ACTING & QUALITY.

EACH FILM DESCRIPTION CONTAINS A SYNOPSIS, A LIST OF GENRES IT BELONGS TO, A LIST OF EMOTIONS IT EXPLORES, SEVEN RATINGS AND A THREE PARAGRAPH REVIEW.

Anthologies of Terror

TALES FROM THE QUADEAD ZONE

1987

A woman tells a ghost two horror stories.

STARS
1/8

STORY
1/8

CREATIVITY
6/8

ACTING
2/8

QUALITY
1/8

REWATCH
1/4

CREEPS
2/4

GIMMICK
3/4

Tales from the Quadead Zone will never be anyone's favorite movie. In fact, it is one of the worst horror anthologies in existence. It is so bad it makes you itchy. It's only quality is that it is so peculiarly directed it makes you wonder if the actors actually got killed to save money, which adds a layer of eeriness. It literally feels like one of these movies that were never meant to be found.

The first segment is about a family with bizarre eating habits. It is highly experimental, has the dramatic presentation of a faux documentary and zero narrative potential. A story has a beginning, middle and end. This isn't a story. The second segment is about a stolen corpse. It has some of the worst dialogue ever written. People constantly swear or talk to themselves.

The audio is cheap. Voices are covered by ambient music. People don't make an effort to compensate by articulating. They say "fuck" and "man" too often, making us wonder if there is an actual script. When they don't, they snigger interminably with a fake, annoying evil laugh. In conclusion, Tales from the Quadead Zone looks and feels like it was directed by someone deaf, dumb and quadriplegic.

Tales of Terror

#53

HOOD OF HORROR

2006

A demon crosses paths with several evil doers and brings them to hell.

  STARS
2/8

 STORY
2/8

CREATIVITY
6/8

 ACTING
5/8

 QUALITY
6/8

 REWATCH
1/4

 CREEPS
3/4

 GIMMICK
3/4

The wraparound story is poorly animated. The segments are confusing. The gore is gratuitous. There is serious overindulgence in unnecessary post-production visual effects. Expect a tremendous amount of slang and foul language. This pretentious production is hard to keep up with and seems like it was written by people filled with anger and pride. Only watch this movie if you love Snoop Dog.

Story 1 is about a frustrated woman who's given voodoo powers and doesn't use them wisely. It lacks morale and has no sense of good and evil. Story 2 is about a racist white couple given an inheritance if they accept to spend a while with black Vietnam veterans. It is dumb and grotesque. Story 3 is about a rapper who gets visited by a woman who can stop time. It is confusing as hell...

When all is said and done, Hood of Horror is, apparently, nothing more than Snoop Dog's business card. He is one of the executive producers and plays the main figure; himself, in the wraparound story. This is basically a vessel for his songs and brand, and a way to polish his image. Let's face it; since you can't be cool and scary at the same time, you usually end up failing on both facets.

WWW.TERROR.CA

Anthologies of Terror

#52

THE ABCS OF DEATH

2012

Death manifests itself 26 different ways all around the world.

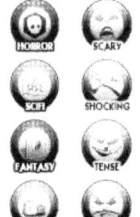

STARS 5/8
STORY 1/8
CREATIVITY 8/8
ACTING 4/8
QUALITY 3/8
REWATCH 1/4
CREEPS 3/4
GIMMICK 4/4

26 filmmakers were offered a decent budget, assigned a letter of the alphabet, asked to choose a corresponding word and to build a short horror story around it. The average segment is 4 to 5 minutes long. Many are subtitled. Half of them revolve around genitals, toilets, abortion, pedophilia, and other controversial subjects, revealing how much the makers care.

The omission of a wrap-around story turns an extreme concept into a lazy gimmick and a mislabeled anthology into a mere compilation. The ABCs of Death adopts many genres, subgenres, and features an impressive collection of monsters, but it is the artistic equivalent of a collective student project. It is emotional charged, very stylistic, but it is extremely vapid.

Sadly, this botched project is everybody's resume killer. It is the intellectual outlet of proud minimalists, not elitists. The premise is interesting, the rules are simple, but ego ruins it all. In order to stand out, most writers persist to steer away from horror, to come up with strange titles; to walk on the edge of their niche, basically. We, the fans, are collateral damage...

Tales of Terror

#51

THE ABCS OF DEATH 2

2014

26 groups of individuals meet dark fates.

  STARS 3/8
  STORY 2/8
  CREATIVITY 8/8
  ACTING 5/8
  QUALITY 4/8
  REWATCH 1/4
  CREEPS 3/4
 GIMMICK 4/4

This sequel beats the original installment by an inch. The wraparound story and most segments are significantly embellished. The editing is generally easier on the eyes, but it doesn't make the extreme marathon feel less like a chore. Most stories are shocking rather than scary. They last about five minutes each, leaving little room for character exposition in most cases.

This said, most creators treat the anthology with respect; an improvement over Part 1. Most shorts make the best of their budget and some pull miracles when it comes to practical and CG effects considering the constraints. The material is mostly exploitative. The weaker stories usually indulge in propaganda. Those political agendas make ABC 2 more serious than necessary.

Some tales rely on irony; others on slapstick humor, but straight dramas work better in most cases, here. Torture, fascists, jail stories and capital punishment are recurring themes, proving once more that creativity is a relative thing that is heavily influenced by the zeitgeist. At least, we don't get too many fecal jokes. Drop your expectations and prepare to be grossed out for two hours!

WWW.TERROR.CA

Anthologies of Terror

SPIRITS OF THE DEAD

1968

Three people meet dark fates.

STARS
3/8
STORY
5/8
CREATIVITY
4/8
ACTING
5/8
QUALITY
6/8
REWATCH
1/4
CREEPS
1/4
GIMMICK
4/4

Spirits of the Dead contains three segments adapted from stories by Edgar All Poe. These short stories are elegant, contain splendid set design and are darkly poetic, but they are also pretentious and extremely vague. Horror anthology films are usually more colorful, more daring, more focused but also simpler. Spirits of the Dead should come with a manual...

The best things about this film are its aesthetics, its occasional nudity, its medieval orgy and its sexual tension. This isn't pornography, though. It's a drama. Spirits of the Dead is rather sluggish. It is way too lengthy. Half of it belongs to the cutting room floor. All stories, at one point or another, lose their destination and wander in useless subplots.

Story one is about a countess who lives a life of promiscuity and debauchery until the day she steps in a trap. Story two is about a murderer who makes money by playing cards and meets an interesting opponent. Story three is about an eccentric actor who wins a Ferrari as a bonus incentive for playing in a film. The question is: will you make it through the three segments or will you zone out?

Tales of Terror

#49

THE MONSTER CLUB

1981

A vampire invites his victim to an eccentric club full of monsters.

STARS
3/8

STORY
3/8

CREATIVITY
5/8

ACTING
5/8

QUALITY
5/8

REWATCH
2/4

CREEPS
2/4

GIMMICK
3/4

This late, weird addition to the Amicus series of anthologies isn't as good as the previous ones. It feels botched. The film has awkward moments that seem to originate from the script. The screenwriters, at times, do come out with their own monsters, but the obligatory vampire shows up to lessen the experience. This film could be more imaginative, indeed.

The wraparound story takes place in a club and the short stories are melodic. Monsters and music are omnipresent, here, in fact, and the equation is weird, to say the least. The uneven comedy is a turn off. We never actually laugh. The actors do their best but struggle with inconsistencies in their characters. The make-up is cheap. The effects are pretty bad.

Fortunately, there are creative surprises at every turn; namely a strange frame by frame animation of a skeleton stripping, a hybrid between two monsters with a powerful whistle and grave-digging ghouls. Don't expect any clever twist or memorable conclusions à la EC Comics. This is arguably the weakest entry in the franchise. It is sadly not up to par.

WWW.TERROR.CA 13

Anthologies of Terror

#48

HORROR HOTEL THE MOVIE

2016

Eerie incidents take place in a decrepit motel.

STARS
4/8
STORY
4/8
CREATIVITY
5/8
ACTING
5/8
QUALITY
5/8
REWATCH
1/4
CREEPS
2/4
GIMMICK
3/4

Horror Hotel the Movie is a horror anthology movie that shares one common element between all its segments; a "motel" and not a "hotel", as alluded to in the title. This film looks incredibly good but is equally amateurish. The wrapping is indeed greater than the filling. We get six stories all compatible in tone and style, and all of them are pretty much as good as the next one.

Segment 1 is about two female aliens descended on earth to repopulate. Segment 2 is about a man who falls in love with a comatose patient. Segment 3 is about a skip-tracer investigating a family of clones suspected of murder. Segment 4 is about an old woman who steals the body of a young one. Segment 5 is about a paraplegic man hired to kill. Segment 6 is about a near future without men.

Horror Hotel the Movie is the compilation of shorts from Horror Hotel: The Webseries. It is nonetheless a consistent production. All segments have very limited casts and stick to one location. Most stories revolve around murder, love, flirt, sex, family and friendship. The dialog is eccentric, the performances are theatrical, the script is decent and the directing has its moments.

Tales of Terror

#47

V/H/S: VIRAL

2014

A cursed video signal triggers a violent crime wave.

STARS 4/8
STORY 4/8
CREATIVITY 6/8
ACTING 5/8
QUALITY 4/8
REWATCH 1/4
CREEPS 3/4
GIMMICK 3/4

V/H/S 2 led us to believe the franchise owners knew what mistakes they originally made and gave us hope that Part 3 takes right back. The found footage format is more a handicap than a crutch, here, because every technical mistake is an excuse for quick editing and unnecessary compositing. The first tale is excellent, but the other two are disorganized, clustered and sadly subpar.

The inclusion of a foreign language in segment two breaks continuity the same way Safe Haven did in Part 2. As an anthology, V/H/S: Viral, much like its title, is a puzzling mishmash on all levels. The wrap-around story is so chaotic it constantly ruins its own twists. It seems everyone; writers, directors and editors especially, has botched their work, leaving us confused and disappointed.

The first and second stories show ambition and creativity, but are polluted by a weak wrap-around story that feels like every other horror movie about a cursed tape. The last short is the weakest link. It lacks narrative, structure, substance and build-up. While V/H/S: Viral expands its mythology between each tale, it never truly ties things together. The sequel just can't handle its gimmick...

WWW.TERROR.CA

Anthologies of Terror

DEADTIME STORIES 2

2011

A storyteller shares three scary supernatural tales.

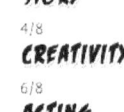

STARS
4/8

STORY
4/8

CREATIVITY
6/8

ACTING
5/8

QUALITY
5/8

REWATCH
1/4

CREEPS
3/4

GIMMICK
3/4

Three more horror stories are introduced by George A Romero in the exact same format as the previous Deadtime Stories. All of them have a supernatural threat for their limited cast to overcome. Their quality varies in terms of narrative structure, continuity, photography and editing. Poor lighting and framing comes as a reminder of the unfavorable sides of short budget filmmaking and inexperience.

There are two bad news for everything good in this. The first story is claustrophobic, plays out like survival horror, but loses its edge towards the end, unable to pull its grand finale. The second one is a confusing thriller, but with a good build-up, that's determined to shock you through taboos. The final story is about a secret scientific experiment gone wrong, about sadness and regrets.

Overall, the shorts feel like junior versions of classic anthologies. "The Gorge" is atmospheric but over-edited and convoluted. "On Sabbath Hill" is suspenseful and compelling but makes bad judgment calls when it comes to scares and subversion. "Dust" starts with a good concept, borrows ideas from many genres, but can't trace a straight line between point A to Z.

Tales of Terror

#45

DEADTIME STORIES

2009

Broadcast on a set of televisions in a dark room, a man narrates three horror stories taken from an old book.

  STARS
4/8

STORY
4/8

CREATIVITY
6/8

ACTING
5/8

QUALITY
5/8

REWATCH
1/4

CREEPS
3/4

GIMMICK
3/4

Deadtime Stories is a collection of three tales combined by a wrap-around segment featuring George A. Romero as himself; in this case a friendly storyteller sitting in a lazy boy. All stories are limited in terms of cast and sets. There isn't visual or tonal uniformity across the different clips, but their structure is similar and they all depict somewhat classic monsters.

The first tale suffers from poor performances, a juvenile script and lack of ambiance. The second tale features a creature that begs to be exploited in horror but never fully was: a siren. It's played for a scare and it's a spine-chilling vision under the right light. We conclude with a cliched, predictable but well shot, tense spiritual procedural.

The two last stories, Wet and House Call, are filmed, framed and directed with more care than the first one. They are also scarier. All shorts are low budget productions with their ups and down. Two stories have a traditional signature twist à la EC Comics, but the other is a little lazy with the finale. Rigor is an issue when it comes to this no more than passable anthology.

WWW.TERROR.CA

17

Anthologies of Terror

THE HOUSE THAT DRIPPED BLOOD

1971

A Scotland Yard inspector investigates an unoccupied house involved in four mysterious cases.

STARS
4/8

STORY
3/8

CREATIVITY
4/8

ACTING
6/8

QUALITY
5/8

REWATCH
2/4

CREEPS
5/4

GIMMICK
3/4

The first two Amicus Portmanteau films had some sort of oracle allowing the narrator to tell the fates of the protagonists. The wrap-around story, here, is a surreal police procedural leading a Scotland Yard inspector to investigate the past of four previous tenants of an old house. The pretext is thin and too serious but you get the same vibe and production value as the previous entries.

You get a segment about an imaginary stalker, one has haunted waxwork, another an evil child and the last deals with a cursed cloak. The ideas are creative but the delivery is flat and the twists badly handled. The thrills aren't there. By standard, we should be surprised at every corner but the film staggers. The acting is not a problem. Some of the familiar faces of the series even show up.

As it is the case with some horror anthology films, the package is more charming than each individual segment. Maybe there's too much vampire stuff and not enough authentic supernatural material with exclusive monster design. With a deceiving wrap around story, this is not a great sequel. It's just another attempt at recreating Dr. Terror's House of Horrors.

Tales of Terror

V/H/S

2012

After trespassing on a private property and vandalizing it, three molesters find and watch a collection of frightening videotapes.

STARS
4/8

STORY
3/8

CREATIVITY
6/8

ACTING
6/8

QUALITY
4/8

REWATCH
2/4

CREEPS
3/4

GIMMICK
3/4

The title makes reference to the videocassettes that created a boom in 80's horror. It's an anthology of five tales, the first of its kind to use nothing but the found footage format and one that is drilled with blatant technological anachronisms. The first short is filmed by a camera mounted on a pair of glasses; the second, third and fifth by a handheld one and the third through web conference.

The wrap around story is in itself a grainy short. Like the other segments, it is of poor visual quality and inexistent cinematography. The frame is shaky enough that it gets away with relatively cheap effects, but something is lost in the process. The cams jumps, falls on the ground and gets splashed with liquid. There are many cuts and some of them are seemingly improvised in post production.

The acting is decent. The protagonists are not so memorable, but the antagonists sure are! Some stories lack ambiance and pacing. On the good side, we are treated with many subgenres and, of course, many twists. As the horror anthology tradition dictates, here the bad guys often get what they deserve. It deals with sex, dating, love, rape and murder, but skillfully shelters in its clever morals.

WWW.TERROR.CA 19

Anthologies of Terror

#42

NIGHT TRAIN TO TERROR

1985

God and Satan discuss the fate of three people aboard a train.

STARS
4/8
STORY
2/8
CREATIVITY
6/8
ACTING
5/8
QUALITY
5/8
REWATCH
2/4
CREEPS
3/4
GIMMICK
4/4

This film is punctuated by songs from a band in a train; some of many uncomfortable moments. God and Satan are on the same train discussing the fate of three people and it is the last thing that we will fully comprehend. The rest is mostly up to our imagination. These three stories are convoluted and so badly edited they raise innumerable unanswered questions and create nothing but confusion.

There's a lot of female nudity in case we get bored or completely lost. At least this is a language we all speak. Like the abundant gore, the nudity is never justified. The shocking elements of this film barely compensate for a horrendous screenplay. Prepare for some of the worst stop motion in film history and a martial art fight so incoherent you'll wish you never pressed 'play'.

Segment one is about a man who is kidnapped and taken to an insane asylum where he is hypnotized and where his mind is controlled. Segment two is about two lovers who join a cult of people fascinated with death. Segment three tells the story of a Satanist dedicated to destroying mankind. These stories are very atmospheric but will require your full attention. You have been warned!

Tales of Terror

#41

TALES OF HALLOWEEN

2015

Evil ruins many people's Halloween celebrations.

STARS
4/8

STORY
3/8

CREATIVITY
8/8

ACTING
7/8

QUALITY
6/8

REWATCH
2/4

CREEPS
3/4

GIMMICK
4/4

Tales of Halloween is a horror film anthology and a collaboration project between artists known for recent success in the low budget independent horror scene. It is a compilation of ten shorts; some good, some bad, but all of them too short for us to really get involved. Two or three stories stand out but most of them have a weak narrative or poor dialog, making them hard to keep up with.

One is about a mean babysitter and her lover; another about a child abducted by the devil. There's the one about evil trick-or-treaters and the one about a summoned demon. There's a segment about a woman haunted by a spirit, then one about a woman who feeds on children. Then, two neighbors compete for the best Halloween decoration. We conclude with a demon child and, finally, man-eating pumpkins.

This anthology is heavily flawed, which is a shame because it is filled with prominent artists from the horror scene. Horror actors, directors and writers play small parts, but nobody can redeem this film. It feels like a draft or a film student's homework. The creators didn't care or communicate enough to make this a homogeneous production. Watch this on Halloween but skip it otherwise.

WWW.TERROR.CA

Anthologies of Terror

#40

NIGHTMARES

1983

Four people experience terrifying moments.

STARS
4/8

STORY
4/8

CREATIVITY
6/8

ACTING
6/8

QUALITY
4/8

REWATCH
2/4

CREEPS
3/4

GIMMICK
4/4

1983's Nightmares is you average, run-of-the-mill horror anthology movie. Its segments have more potential than what we end up with, mainly due to the poor screenplay and the way they were directed. The camera is shaky, the dialogue is boring, sometimes mumbled, there is hesitation in the blocking of characters and the suspense is not structured effectively. The effects are pretty bad, too.

Emilio Estevez and Lance Henriksen deserve better than this and both wish they were elsewhere. Estevez is stuck in a story that's ahead of its time and will not age well. Lance Henriksen is the star of a story with no gimmick that you won't remember by the time the end credits roll. And that's the main problem with this film. It is okay but certainly not memorable.

Segment one is about an escape mental patient suspected of committing a series of murders. Segment two is the story of an obsessed video game player who breaks the limits of an arcade machine. Segment three is about a priest who is tormented by an aggressive driver. Segment four is about a woman who suspects her house is infested with rats. Sounds fun? It almost is!

Tales of Terror

#39

TRAPPED ASHES

2006

Tourists visiting Hollywood become locked inside a horror museum.

STARS 4/8
STORY 4/8
CREATIVITY 6/8
ACTING 6/8
QUALITY 6/8
REWATCH 2/4
CREEPS 3/4
GIMMICK 4/4

What happens when you ask masters of horror to direct four poorly written scripts? Well, you might end up with a passable horror anthology film called Trapped Ashes. This picture is reminiscent of the Hammer Amicus Portmanteau franchise. A bunch of strangers are united in unexpected circumstances and must each tell a scary tale to make the wraparound story move forward. The ending is predictable.

Segment one is about a woman whose new breast implants feed on human blood. It is darkly erotic and very immature. Segment two is about a woman's lover who comes back from death to have sex with her. It has style but no substance. Story three is fascinating and depends solely on dialog and performances. Story four is about a tape worm endangering a pregnant woman's fetus.

All stories revolve around sex and all are equally gory. All stories are both supernatural and surreal. All stories start oddly and get better only to confuse us by the end. They are well shot, well lit, but they feel experimental and could use some structure. Most effects are well done but the 3-D can get on one's nerve. The wraparound story's pretext is one of the weakest I've seen.

WWW.TERROR.CA

Anthologies of Terror

TORTURE GARDEN

1967

Four people get their dark potential futures told by a wax statue.

STARS
4/8

STORY
4/8

CREATIVITY
6/8

ACTING
6/8

QUALITY
5/8

REWATCH
3/4

CREEPS
3/4

GIMMICK
3/4

Second release in the Amicus Portmanteau horror anthology movie franchise, and unfortunately not as lively or gimmicky as Dr. Terror's House of Horrors was. Torture Garden still means well and delivers four dark tales told telepathically by the wax representation of a Sybil to a bunch of characters looking for something sensational. Like them, we want a good show and that's mostly what we get!

The performances, the lighting, the ambiance and the sets are generally living up to the previous film. The same thing cannot be said of the camera work, which isn't always filming the right thing right at the right time. The stories themselves are hits and misses. Two of them are deliberate Edgar Allan Poe references and the two others about love and lust. There's an obvious lack of rigor, here.

Some twists work better than others. The wraparound story is fun to come back to in between each segment and contains its own surprises. The directing isn't exactly meticulous but the production doesn't suffer much from it. The main issues remain the laziness of the script and a lack of eye candy. You'll still have a good time with this if you're not too picky.

Tales of Terror

#37

AFTER MIDNIGHT

1989

A teacher invites some of his students to his home for private lessons about fears.

STARS
4/8

STORY
5/8

CREATIVITY
4/8

ACTING
6/8

QUALITY
6/8

REWATCH
3/4

CREEPS
3/4

GIMMICK
3/4

A teacher wants to break down the rudiments of fear as a survival mechanism and tells three horrifying stories to his students to make his point. The first is about a couple who take refuge in a scary house after their car broke down. The second is about four girls who run into a crazy gas attendant and his dogs. The last story is about a receptionist who gets stalked by a creep on the phone.

The wraparound story starts interestingly but eventually runs out of momentum. Its existence ends up being more or less justified. The three segments have limited casts and sets. The actors are decent. The casting is fine. In fact, every aspect of this film is no more or less than decent. The directing is minimal and so is the writing. The dialog isn't realistic but it gets the story across.

All stories are plausible, so don't expect supernatural elements. All stories are realistic thrillers. They have solid build-up, crescendo suspense but boring and predictable endings. The same can be said about the wraparound tale. So After Midnight is not the best horror anthology movie ever made, but there is far worse out there. Fans of theses should definitely give it a try.

WWW.TERROR.CA   25

Anthologies of Terror

#36

HOLIDAYS

2016

Eight dark stories based on Holidays are told in chronological order.

STARS
5/8
STORY
5/8
CREATIVITY
7/8
ACTING
6/8
QUALITY
6/8
REWATCH
1/4
CREEPS
3/4
GIMMICK
4/4

This comes out in a time when horror anthology movies are trendy. Most anthologies of the 2010's are written and directed by many artists and, like Holidays, most have uniformity issues for this reason. Some of the segments are darker than others, some are downright comedies, some are art-house and some are experimental. By thinking outside the box, most segments end up being deeply confusing.

Valentine's Day is good but should've been longer. St Patrick's Day is a mind fuck that's too weird for most audiences. Easter is frightening and will make you remember what it is to be scared as a child. Mother's day is vague and unsatisfying. Father's Day is unmemorable. Halloween is the best of the bunch. It will make you cringe! Christmas is a dark delight and New Year's Eve is... alright.

All segments are well shot and most actors are convincing, but the scripts are generally flawed. The main problem is not the segments themselves, but how short they are and their inability to set the mood. The second issue with most stories is that they are not quintessential renditions of their respective themes. With a title like Holidays, we'd expect simpler stories with stronger gimmicks.

Tales of Terror

#35

V/H/S/2

2013

Two private investigators stumble upon a collection of videotapes containing the supernatural deaths of different individuals

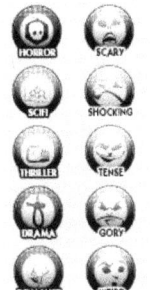

STARS
5/8

STORY
5/8

CREATIVITY
7/8

ACTING
6/8

QUALITY
4/8

REWATCH
2/4

CREEPS
3/4

GIMMICK
3/4

This sequel to the shaky V/H/S is now visually tolerable. The scenes are paced better and the shorts don't rely as much on clustering transitions. Like the original, V/H/S 2 is a horror anthology entirely shot under the non-spoken rules of found footage films. This includes the wrap-around story. The special effects are better, supernatural by the nature of the script and therefore more ambitious.

Every short is gory, controversial, sexy, and probably contains nudity. The creativity level has been cranked up a notch. Aside from a breath-taking third story that goes in all sorts of directions, the material, here, is simple enough and deals with types of monsters we, the viewer, have a heard of. You get ghosts, zombies, demons and aliens, namely.

Though seemingly made for people who appreciated Amicus, Creepshow, Trilogy of Terror and other popular anthologies, it lacks the uniformity, attention to detail and rudimentary skills that made the classics legendary. On the other hand, the makers are experienced and know what they are doing. We're seemingly surfing on a stagnant subgenre that, by definition, isn't expensive, yet scary.

WWW.TERROR.CA

Anthologies of Terror

CHILLERAMA
2011

A drive-in theater presents different short horror films

STARS
5/8

STORY
4/8

CREATIVITY
6/8

ACTING
6/8

QUALITY
6/8

REWATCH
2/4

CREEPS
2/4

GIMMICK
4/4

The first segment, Wadzilla, is hilarious, imaginative and disgusting. It tells the story of a man whose sperm grows increasingly bigger and gets out of control. Segment two is a musical homoerotic short about a teenager who questions his sexual orientation. Segment three is the Nazi version of Frankenstein and is shot entirely in German. Segment four pays homage to old zombie flicks.

Each story was composed and directed by individual artists, none are more than decent. The dialog is alright. The effects are interesting but more amusing than realistic. The humor is generally immature and sometimes feel like inside jokes by high school students. The acting is the best aspect of the compilation. The wrap around story intertwines beautifully. The package is nice, indeed...

All tales have a particular aesthetic taken care of in post-production. This is also part of Chillerama's charm. The problem with the film is that its various styles conceal poor stories and several sexual jokes that just never hit their mark. This is a good attempt at taking the horror anthology film elsewhere, but it obviously takes more than imagination and intention to deliver a good product.

Tales of Terror

PATIENT SEVEN

2016

A psychiatrist interrogates six dangerous mental patients as part of research for his new book.

STARS 5/8
STORY 4/8
CREATIVITY 7/8
ACTING 6/8
QUALITY 6/8
REWATCH 2/4
CREEPS 3/4
GIMMICK 4/4

Patient Seven is a horror anthology film that contains seven segments and a wraparound story. It lasts a little less than two hours, which is a decent amount of time for each story. Some are extremely short and some stretch for too long. This is a quality production that is fun to sit through despite a few annoyances. The actors are mostly convincing and the cinematography always professional.

Story 1 is about a creature that visits a woman and her child at night. Story 2 is about a murderer who carries a body on Halloween night. Story 3 is about a man who goes scavenging during a zombie apocalypse. Story 4 is about a child who makes money off of a swear jar. In story 5, a teenager attempts to exorcise her sister. Story 6 is about a vampire hunter and story 7 has... more zombies!

Michael Ironside coats everything here in sugar. This film is not terrible, but it is a patchwork. The characters in the wrap around story, for instance, are played by different, younger actors in the individual segments. It becomes apparent that this odd scheme allowed seven teams to work independently, but the end result is confusing. What's more, the end of the movie is very predictable.

WWW.TERROR.CA

Anthologies of Terror

#32

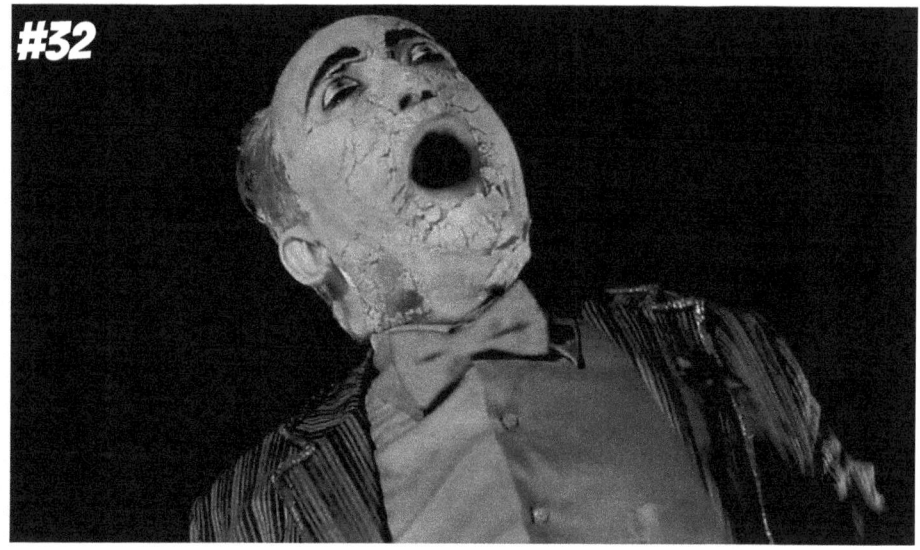

THE THEATRE BIZARRE

2011

A woman is attracted to a deserted theater where an impresario entertains her.

STARS 5/8
STORY 4/8
CREATIVITY 7/8
ACTING 6/8
QUALITY 6/8
REWATCH 2/4
CREEPS 3/4
GIMMICK 4/4

With its extremely atmospheric wraparound story and six highly imaginative segments, The Theatre Bizarre sets itself apart from the usual horror anthology film. As the title indicates, these tales are not only dark but all bizarre. Some have non-linear narratives. Some rely heavily on editing to make their point. Some are nasty mindfucks. Anything goes.

Most actors do a fine job. The always unsettling Udo Kier and the ethereal Virginia Newcomb play mesmerizing roles in the framing segments. Some of the short stories are created by people who have made their marks in the horror industry. They know what they are doing. Sadly, the others appear to be experimenting. The cinematography is, in all cases, superior.

Many segments are about love, jealousy, cheating, deviant sex, that thin barrier between sex and horror. All of them are either surreal or supernatural. The stories that rely the most on editing are the ones that fail. They fail to create suspense and generate confusion instead. The first half of the anthology contains the better segments, making the second half hard to sit through.

Tales of Terror

DARK TALES OF JAPAN

2004

A bus passenger insists on telling the driver five frightening stories.

STARS
5/8

STORY
4/8

CREATIVITY
7/8

ACTING
6/8

QUALITY
6/8

REWATCH
2/4

CREEPS
3/4

GIMMICK
4/4

Dark Tales of Japan is an interesting collection of five stories written and directed by the cream of the crop of Japanese horror masters. Some stories are shorter than others, some are significantly better than others, but, as a whole, this is a memorable horror anthology film that induces shivers and doesn't rely on cheap jump scares. These stories contain little suspense but are still scary.

The first segment is a journalistic procedural about a "spiderwoman" who haunts a highway. In the second segment, a man tapes every corner of a house to repel a spirit. The third segment is about a woman haunted by childhood memories. The fourth one tells the story of a man who develops an obsession for blondes. The final segment is about a man who gets stuck in an elevator.

The wraparound story is super creepy. It involves a bus passenger who insists on telling five legends to the driver. The tales are generally well-paced. The longer stories are more involving, of course, but they sometimes drag for so long that they become predictable. Some stories have nested narrators or non-linear scripts. This becomes a double-edged sword. This film hits and misses.

WWW.TERROR.CA

Anthologies of Terror

#30

CRADLE OF FEAR

2001

A mysterious man sows pain and death wherever he goes.

STARS
5/8

STORY
5/8

CREATIVITY
6/8

ACTING
6/8

QUALITY
6/8

REWATCH
2/4

CREEPS
3/4

GIMMICK
4/4

Right out of a mad man's mind, it feels, Cradle of Fear is a collection of four tales and a wraparound story filled with shock, sex and gore. The wraparound story is a police procedural that intertwines with the segments. We come to understand that the archvillain unifies all stories. He is some kind of reaper, though this is never confirmed. All we really know is that he has supernatural powers.

The first segment is about a woman who has sex with him while doing hard drugs. The second half of the story is her bad trip. Segment two tells the story of two thieves who break into the wrong house at the wrong time. Segment three is about an amputee who kills someone and steals his leg. The last segment is about a man who becomes obsessed by a snuff website.

The film doesn't have the best photography and has obnoxious editing techniques. The generic sound of blades chopping flesh is irritating. The cheap techno score is torture. It completely destroys any attempt at suspense. On the plus side, the prosthetic make-up and special effects will send shivers down your spine. If it's boobs and red sauce you want, then look no further.

Tales of Terror

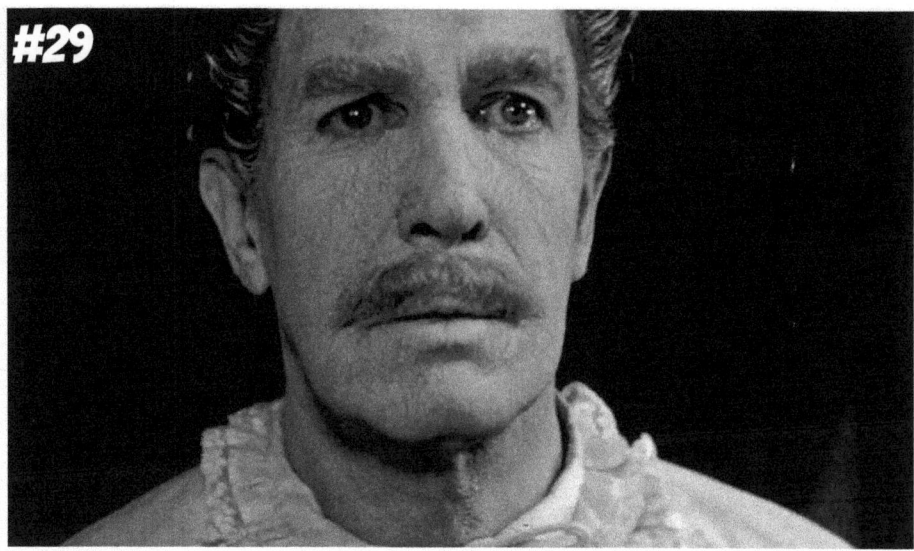

#29

TALES OF TERROR

1962

A man presents three stories of shock and horror.

STARS
5/8

STORY
5/8

CREATIVITY
6/8

ACTING
6/8

QUALITY
6/8

REWATCH
2/4

CREEPS
2/4

GIMMICK
4/4

Tales of Terror is a horror anthology film in which each segment is introduced via voice-over narration by Vincent Price, who also appears in all three narratives. All stories are period pieces and all are of theatrical acting style. The casts are limited in size and the sets are gorgeous but equally restricted. This is a dialogue driven compilation of dark tales.

Classy, classic, cruel, comedic; Tales of Terror has Vincent Price drinking alcohol in all three stories and spelling out every plot detail. One of the film's best features is its photography. It is precise, always colorful, shiny and beautifully textured. The set design is uncanny. Some of the special effects are particularly well integrated but some fail to impress.

Segment one is about a woman who visits her estranged father and stirs up old memories. Segment two, the comedic one, is about a vengeful cuckolded man who entombs his wife and her lover in his basement. Segment three tells the story of a hypnotist who prolongs the moments of a man's death. All three tales are equally interesting and masterfully directed.

WWW.TERROR.CA

Anthologies of Terror

#28

FROM A WHISPER TO A SCREAM

1987

An historian tells four horror stories to a reporter.

STARS
5/8

STORY
5/8

CREATIVITY
7/8

ACTING
5/8

QUALITY
5/8

REWATCH
2/4

CREEPS
3/4

GIMMICK
4/4

From a Whisper to a Scream is a collection of four frightening stories, all with a strong air of dread and tension throughout, with little to no resting time. This kind of pacing makes the film somewhat depressing but oh so sinister. The shorts are compressed, so things feel a little rushed. They are all filmed in impersonal ways. We don't buy the various love stories. We don't feel the sadness.

The shooting techniques are rough around the edges. The editing is as tight as the runtime needs it to be, which hinders build-up. The segments are genuinely creepy, but they take a while to sink into the audience. The twists are interesting. The writers' moral compass is on and off when it comes to conclusions. We don't always get a satisfying ending but we always get a surprise.

In the first segment, a man attempts to date his boss and gets in trouble. In the second one, an injured man discovers that his rescuer knows the formula to eternal life and wants to steal it. Segment three is about a circus glass eater who falls in love with someone from his audience. Segment four is about a handful of soldiers that get captured by crippled children.

Tales of Terror

THE VAULT OF HORROR

1973

Five strangers meet in a gentlemen's club and tell each other their recurring nightmares.

STARS
5/8

STORY
4/8

CREATIVITY
6/8

ACTING
6/8

QUALITY
5/8

REWATCH
3/4

CREEPS
3/4

GIMMICK
3/4

The Vault of Horror is just as creative as the most eccentric entries of the Amicus anthology collection. Based on EC Comics, like 1972's Tales from the Crypt, it finds the perfect balance of fright and fun and delivers it using bright colors and lively dialog. The stories all feature both social and supernatural horror, and bad guys that bite the dust by the time twists are revealed.

There's something in this for all horror fan segmentations. It namely tells the stories of cursed artifacts, dark talents and voodoo spells. It tackles many subgenres but has a preference for the occult. Anyone up to date with the franchise will see the wrap around story's conclusion coming from a mile away but it is a necessary evil because it gives depth to each segment and feels continuous.

The practical effects are breath-taking. Inanimate objects are so skillfully rigged and animated that their temper, their mood and their personality comes across. The Vault of Horror learns from the previous sequel; Tales from the Crypt, yet it ends up hiding in its shadow. In fact, all stories have great gimmicks but some of them simply require less eye-candy to tell their arc.

WWW.TERROR.CA 35

Anthologies of Terror

CREEPSHOW III

2006

The dark supernatural fates of different individuals intertwine.

STARS
5/8

STORY
4/8

CREATIVITY
7/8

ACTING
5/8

QUALITY
4/8

REWATCH
3/4

CREEPS
3/4

GIMMICK
3/4

We're greeted with a cheap and very disappointing tween animated intro that screams amateurism and laziness. It replaces the much better transitions and shaded frame-by-frame animation the previous film had with nothing worth trading for. The wrap around story is nowhere to be found. It is replaced by an unconventional structure and a nonlinear storyline.

Tough often amusing or gory, it doesn't measure up to the rigor and artistic genius of the previous ones. In fact, it doesn't even try. Any hope for continuity in style, production quality, acting, writing and directing will be quickly turned down. While the different segments introduce interesting ideas, they don't belong in one of the best anthology franchise ever made.

This isn't The Twilight Zone, but the different tales and threats featured reveal an obvious influence. Alternate dimensions and travel in time and space are big themes, here. As far as antagonists, you get an irradiated schoolgirl decomposing iteratively, a mind-controlling genie-like radio, a sex-driven serial killer, a suspicious wife and the ghost of a homeless man.

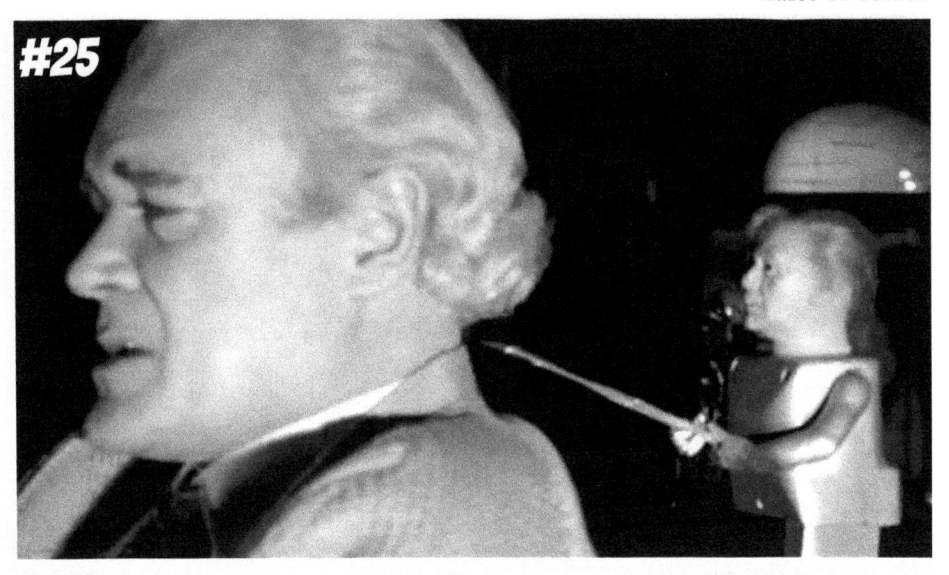

Tales of Terror

#25

ASYLUM

1972

As a test for an interview, a psychiatrist examines four patients locked into the rooms of an asylum.

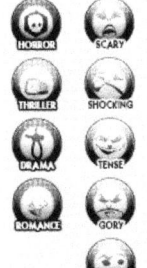

STARS
5/8

STORY
5/8

CREATIVITY
6/8

ACTING
6/8

QUALITY
5/8

REWATCH
3/4

CREEPS
3/4

GIMMICK
3/4

This franchise varies in its ability to grab the audience's attention and keep it. It succeeds in doing so when the wraparound story is fun enough, dark enough, and leads us to segments of quality with incredible twists and a good build-up. Asylum isn't the best nor the worst of Amicus' collection of anthologies. It suffers from its past mistakes but benefits from what it learned to do well.

We get a possessed doll, revenants, animated severed limbs and a bit of psychological horror on top of the supernatural element for good measure. The stories range from entertaining to boring. By tradition, all stories end with an unpredictable twist. As always, the acting, the photography, the lighting, the costumes and the set design are strong aspects.

Two of the tales in this anthology are particularly creepy visually. The effects are minimal but effective. Those short segments are meant to trade time normally dedicated to character exposition for chills and shorter arcs, which is handled brilliantly here. Asylum's main problem, as usual, is its weaker segments. Those quality productions are sometimes sadly overlooked.

WWW.TERROR.CA

Anthologies of Terror

#24

QUICKSILVER HIGHWAY

1997

A travelling showman tells horror stories to the people he meets.

STARS 5/8
STORY 5/8
CREATIVITY 6/8
ACTING 6/8
QUALITY 6/8
REWATCH 3/4
CREEPS 3/4
GIMMICK 3/4

Quicksilver Highway is a compilation of two stories; one by Stephen King and the second one by Clive Barker. So, we basically have short story adaptations from the two most popular modern horror authors in the world. How can this go wrong? Well, Mick Garris is directing. He's known for pulling miracles with small budgets, but most of his work has a made for TV look and feel and it's a problem.

This means we get grade B actors, special effects, sets, costumes, editing, and a general sense that this was shot quickly. Make no mistake, Quicksilver Highway is still better than most horror anthology movies out there. It is the ambiance that is unappealing. The humor is odd. The score is cheap and certainly not tense and scary, as it should be.

The wraparound story features a creepy Christopher Lloyd telling two horror tales. The first one is about a man who picks up a hitchhiker and soon regrets it. Story two is about another man whose hands rebel against him. Both segments are interesting but not excellent. The first one is very creative but the second one reminds us of things we've seen a millions times in horror movies.

Tales of Terror

#23

FROM BEYOND THE GRAVE

1974

Four people acquire enchanted items from an antique store.

STARS
5/8

STORY
6/8

CREATIVITY
7/8

ACTING
6/8

QUALITY
6/8

REWATCH
3/4

CREEPS
3/4

GIMMICK
3/4

Visually appealing and containing some of the best horror segments of its franchise, From Beyond the Grave is an aggregation of highly creative shorts that intertwine with a wrap-around story involving all main protagonists successively visiting an antique store owned by a mysterious man. They each reveal an intrinsic ounce of evil, and therefore possibly deserve what's coming to them...

So far, this twisted narrative is one of the most effective in the franchise. All tales center on relationships and human vice and all trigger events reside in a magical item bought or stolen. This at least guarantees a steady element of paranormal across the different shorts, along with continuous surreal humor. Indeed, this is a masterpiece in writing and directing.

The pacing of the story is just right, with no moments of boredom even when dialog leads the way. Well shot and lit, low on gore and lively instead, From Beyond the Grave, 7th and not the least of the Amicus Portmanteau movies, is an oil painting in motion. It contains great performances, delivers a layered script, immerses with peculiar set design then surprises with hectic special effects.

WWW.TERROR.CA

Anthologies of Terror

#22

DR. TERROR'S HOUSE OF HORRORS
1965

Five strangers boarding a train have their fortune told by a man offering tarot readings.

STARS 5/8
STORY 6/8
CREATIVITY 7/8
ACTING 7/8
QUALITY 5/8
REWATCH 3/4
CREEPS 3/4
GIMMICK 3/4

Here are five imaginative tales and a wraparound story that will creep up on you. Each story has a defining supernatural element to it and each will have you follow a flawed protagonist who pays for his sins by the time the story ends. The wraparound story gets increasingly darker and will send a shiver down your spine with its dramatic conclusion.

Voodoo, severed limbs, plants; no special effect, no matter how cinematically challenging, seems too hard to bring to screen. Some stories fall flat but some are simply delightful. The segments are uniform in tone and style, though, and the good performances make them exciting despite some screenplay weaknesses. This is the ultimate cinematographic buffet.

The visual effects are visionary and grandiose yet minimalist. Although simple, often quickly shown and usually hidden in darkness or shadows, their level of complexity makes them exquisite. The fact that they are at the center of the stories makes them greater accomplishments. They were required by the script from the get go and could've gone terribly wrong but didn't. Kudos.

Tales of Terror

#21

TWISTS OF TERROR

1997

While sorting through piles of newspaper clippings, an odd man tells three creepy stories.

STARS
5/8

STORY
5/8

CREATIVITY
4/8

ACTING
6/8

QUALITY
6/8

REWATCH
3/4

CREEPS
3/4

GIMMICK
4/4

Nothing is ever as it seems in Twists of Terror. We get three demented tales that end in irony, some with multiple twists. Twist of Terror's signature is that it stays away from supernatural elements and focuses on human relationships, instead, adding a drop of surrealism where needed. These stories are somewhat unmemorable but in fact highly rewatchable for this reason.

The first story is about a couple whose car breaks down and whose bad fortune quickly spirals out of control. The second one is about a man who gets bitten by a dog and seeks medical help in a nearby hospital. The last one is about a woman whose life revolves around flirting and dating. All segments are equally entertaining and share a certain vibe.

This Canadian horror anthology has a conservative approach. Its stories are compelling, its actors interesting, but it doesn't rely on big stunts or special effects. It is also relatively low on gore. It doesn't even have the luxury of a complex wraparound segment, but we do get a narrator in between each tale doing his best to glue all this together.

WWW.TERROR.CA

Anthologies of Terror

#20

BLACK SABBATH

1963

A man tells three frightening stories.

STARS
5/8

STORY
5/8

CREATIVITY
6/8

ACTING
7/8

QUALITY
6/8

REWATCH
3/4

CREEPS
3/4

GIMMICK
4/4

Boris Karloff presents three stories. The Drop of Water is about a woman who steals a ring from a corpse and soon regrets it. The Telephone is about a woman who receives menacing phone calls from someone she believes is dead. The Wurdalak is a vampire story. This is a superior horror anthology film you won't want to miss if you are a completist. It is directed by master of horror Mario Bava.

While the stories themselves are not always well written, Mario Bava ensures a superb photography. His cinematography is composed of intricate lighting, rich, textured set design and suspense created out of thin air. His brilliant use of sound induces shivers. The Drop of Water is particularly frightening and probably the best segment. It encompasses the best elements of this presentation.

It'll suck you in from the first moments. When you're not scared, you will either be thrilled or amazed. Two of the three stories are period pieces, which may or may not rub you the right way. There is gore but only a necessary amount. Bava relies on atmosphere, here, and works his magic by giving an aesthetic to stories that wouldn't otherwise get our attention.

Tales of Terror

#19

TERROR TRACT

2000

A pushy real estate agent tries to convince his clients to buy properties with dark histories.

STARS
5/8

STORY
5/8

CREATIVITY
6/8

ACTING
7/8

QUALITY
7/8

REWATCH
3/4

CREEPS
3/4

GIMMICK
4/4

Terror Tract is one of the rare instances, in horror anthology films, where the wraparound story is better than the segments themselves. The wraparound story is about a pushy real estate agent trying to convince his clients, a happy couple, to buy one of his properties. The real estate agent is played by John Ritter at his best. He plays a key role that constantly evolves.

Segment one, we weakest one, is about a man who finds out his wife is cheating on him and exacts revenge. Segment two is the most interesting one. It tells the story of an evil monkey adopted by a suburban family. Segment three is about a troubled psychic who meets a therapist to tell her about visions he has. This is the shortest tale and the darkest one.

Directing surpasses screenwriting, here. The stories aren't that interesting on paper and don't get much better on screen, but they at least hold our attention. Good acting makes us forgive the many pitfalls Terror Tract runs right into. Terror Tract doesn't have the benefits of high budget productions. Its sets and casts are limited. As an horror anthology, though, it is above average.

WWW.TERROR.CA

Anthologies of Terror

#18

TALES FROM THE HOOD

1995

A funeral home owner tells three drug dealers the last stories of his recent customers.

STARS 5/8
STORY 5/8
CREATIVITY 7/8
ACTING 6/8
QUALITY 6/8
REWATCH 3/4
CREEPS 3/4
GIMMICK 4/4

Tales from the Hood is annoying when it gets political or spiritual, but is highly enjoyable when it sticks to gore and the supernatural. Because all four segments are from the same two creators, there is noticeable uniformity in the photography and overall tone. Racial supremacy is an obvious concern for screenwriters Rusty Cundieff and Darin Scott. It is a recurring theme, here. Not subtle...

The first segment is straight to the point and so simple-minded that it needs to complicate itself to meet its running time. The second one gets lost in its symbolism but is a good excuse for cool practical effects. The third segment is by far the best. It meets an unspoken rule of horror anthologies and features killer dolls. The last story is a torture seance taking place in prison.

The most interesting thing to notice, here, is that in most of the tales, the protagonist is a bad guy or someone who repents. Cops are painted as unidimensional, arrogant, violent and evil, while black people are depicted as martyrs. The language used is rough and sometimes hurtful. Sadly, Tales from the Hood condemns racism but somehow perpetrates what it denounces.

Tales of Terror

#17

THE WILLIES

1990

Two brothers and their cousin tell each other spooky stories.

STARS
5/8

STORY
5/8

CREATIVITY
8/8

ACTING
5/8

QUALITY
6/8

REWATCH
3/4

CREEPS
3/4

GIMMICK
4/4

In The Willies, two brothers and their cousin tell each other scary stories inside a tent at night. They start off with three quick urban legends to set the mood. Then, ten minutes in, they get to the two main segments of the anthology. Segment one is every bullied teenager's wet dream; a tale about a vengeful toilet monster you won't soon forget. Segment two is about a boy obsessed with flies.

Most characters are children or tweens. The target audience is young, so the gore is minimal but it's there. The editing is botched, the acting is horrendous, there are serious pacing issues, the dialogue is pretty bad and the morales of the segments are highly questionable, but the film is somehow entertaining regardless. In the end, these feel like adaptations of horror novellas for teenagers.

Sometimes a thriller, sometimes repugnant, sometimes a monster movie and sometimes a comedy, The Willies never really finds its tone. It doesn't even manage to remain politically correct and can hardly be recommended to kids. Mutants strangle teenagers, teachers piss blood, revenants get dismembered and parents give up on raising their psychotic child. It's all in here, kiddos!

WWW.TERROR.CA   45

Anthologies of Terror

#16

A CHRISTMAS HORROR STORY
2015

Christmas night turns into mayhem for different people.

STARS 5/8
STORY 5/8
CREATIVITY 8/8
ACTING 7/8
QUALITY 7/8
REWATCH 3/4
CREEPS 3/4
GIMMICK 4/4

After an enthralling opening credit scene with impressive 3-D effects that makes us presume we're in good hands, we are introduced to William Shatner who will play the part of a radio host who works the graveyard shift on Christmas night. He is more or less connected to the four stories included in this horror anthology film. In fact, all segments cut back and forth, and some intertwine.

The first story is about teenagers investigating two murders that occurred in their school's basement. The second story is about a couple whose child becomes bizarre after getting lost in the woods. Story three is about a family hunted by Krampus, a Christmas demon. Story 4 is about a plague that strikes Santa Claus' village. The way tales overlap creates condensed build up à la Trick 'r Treat.

Nobody here is having a merry Christmas except us. This film is likely to become a season favorite for horror fans. You can count on talented actors to keep you on the edge of your seat all the way through. They give it all they've got and so did the writers and directors. This is an anthology film of superior quality in a sea of video on demand flops.

Tales of Terror

#15

SOUTHBOUND

2015

Different people die in related ways.

STARS 6/8
STORY 5/8
CREATIVITY 7/8
ACTING 7/8
QUALITY 7/8
REWATCH 2/4
CREEPS 3/4
GIMMICK 4/4

Southbound is a horror anthology film with a level of production quality we haven't seen in a while. The creators of V/H/S raised the bar higher than before and Southbound is the end product. Things start scary, tense and heavy but shift two gears down by the time the first segment starts to let us breath. In fact, we get some kind of a wraparound story and three segments in between.

The wraparound segment is one story split in the middle. The other ones are somewhat tied together. One ends where another one starts. Story zero is about two men running from the reaper. Story one is about three women invited to a strange supper. Story two is about a man who attempts to save the life of a woman he ran over with his car. Story three is about a man looking for his missing sister.

The screenwriters and directors of this film took a lot of interesting decisions that are rarely intuitive. As an example, all segments rely on each other to feel like complete stories. Considering this challenge, it feels like communication flowed well between the different teams on paper and on set. There isn't an obvious shift in tone from one segment to another. A lot of talent went into this.

WWW.TERROR.CA

Anthologies of Terror

#14

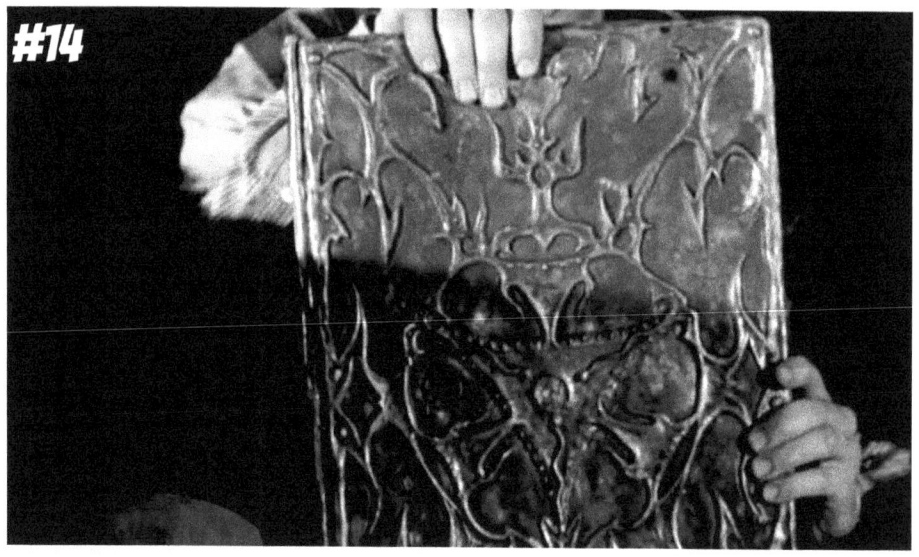

NECRONOMICON

1993

A famous writer trespasses in the catacombs of a monastery to read the pages of a sacred book.

STARS
6/8

STORY
6/8

CREATIVITY
8/8

ACTING
7/8

QUALITY
6/8

REWATCH
3/4

CREEPS
4/4

GIMMICK
6/4

Few filmmakers have managed to faithfully depict H.P. Lovecraft's world on screen. How do you describe the indescribable? How do you name the unnamable? How do you make sense of it all and come up with a fascinating and comprehensible story? The makers walk a thin line but the end product is accessible, which is a tour de force. Lovecraft was never "accessible"....

Necronomicon is the "book the dead". It is also the name of a horror anthology film composed of three segments and a wraparound story. Segment one is about a man who brings his family back to life using the book. Segment two is about a woman rescued from her abusive stepfather by a strange scientist. The last segment is about a cop searching for her missing partner after their car crashed.

The worst aspect of this film is that it so packed with information it is hard to follow. Things get clearer upon rewatch and, fortunately, the whole film gets better the more you watch it. Each of these segments could be feature films. They don't particularly rely on a twist, contrary to most horror anthology film segments, and they pretty much all have three arcs.

Tales of Terror

#13

AMUSEMENT

2008

Three women share a dark fate.

STARS
6/8

STORY
5/8

CREATIVITY
5/8

ACTING
7/8

QUALITY
7/8

REWATCH
3/4

CREEPS
3/4

GIMMICK
4/4

Amusement is one of the best horror anthology movies to feature plausible content exclusively. The wrap around story is smart. It blends gradually and seamlessly. A few screenwriters have attempted this in recent years but rarely with so much tact and such good pacing. Amusement was directed by someone who definitely knows what he's doing and was written just as brilliantly.

There are three segments, here. The first is about a couple on a road trip who accept to travel in a convoy and soon regret their choice. The second is about a babysitter who is terrorized by a human-size clown doll that may be alive. The last one tells the story of a couple who go looking for their missing friend inside a hotel whose owner they find suspicious.

The killer, AKA "The Laugh", is played by an unrecognizable Keir O'Donnell, who proved to be a true chameleon. He is unidentifiable, even in plain sight. He sometimes wears prosthetics or is otherwise filmed in a way to partially conceal his face. This is a visual challenge whose success is hard to predict on paper, so the film deserves to be praised for it.

WWW.TERROR.CA

Anthologies of Terror

#12

TWO EVIL EYES

1990

Two stories of twisted romance by Edgar Allan Poe are presented.

STARS
6/8

STORY
5/8

CREATIVITY
6/8

ACTING
7/8

QUALITY
6/8

REWATCH
3/4

CREEPS
3/4

GIMMICK
4/4

Two Evil Eyes is composed of two relatively short segments inspired by Edgar Allen Poe's work. One is called The Facts in the Case of Mr. Valdemar and the other The Black Cat. The two stories were previously adapted many times, namely in 1962 horror anthology film Tales of Terror. You'd think that at an hour each these simple stories would resort to filler. In fact, we don't feel an extrapolation.

George A. Romero is the mastermind behind the first segment in which a woman plots her husband's death along with her secret lover. Dario Argento handles the second segment; the story of a photographer who tortures a black cat and gets bad karma in return. Both stories are twisted romances. Both stories have a supernatural element to them and a surreal ambiance.

The actors give decent performances. The writing is slightly poetic and the directing limited to a few players and sets. We haven't really seen this kind of format in horror anthologies much up to now, that is the hour long attempt, and the end result is rather refreshing. This is first and foremost a celebration of Edgar Allen Poes's talent by two no less talented contemporary masters of horror.

Tales of Terror

BODY BAGS

1993

A coroner tells the dark stories of three corpses.

STARS 6/8
STORY 6/8
CREATIVITY 7/8
ACTING 7/8
QUALITY 7/8
REWATCH 3/4
CREEPS 3/4
GIMMICK 4/4

John Carpenter plays an amusing, creepy-looking coroner in the wraparound story of this above average horror anthology film. He also shares the directing tasks with Tobe Hooper and Larry Sulkis. Many more horror icons and popular actors join us for three super atmospheric segments. These shorts have the production value of medium to high budget horror films.

Segment one is a compressed whodunit slasher taking place in and around a gas station at night. Segment two, more comedic, makes fun of magical solutions to hair loss. Segment three is about a man who receives an eye transplant after losing one in a violent car accident and who then gets vision from the dead. All three stories are equally well written and shot. All stories are memorable.

Directed with dynamism, ambiance, pacing, perfect cinematography and special effects ahead of their time, Body Bags has one realistic tale, a science-fiction one and one from the grave. They are so entertaining that you won't be able to pick a favorite one. The planets sure aligned for what turns out to be one of the most interesting horror anthology films ever made.

WWW.TERROR.CA

Anthologies of Terror

#10

TALES FROM THE CRYPT

1972

Five people meet a crypt guardian who has a story for each of them.

STARS
6/8

STORY
6/8

CREATIVITY
7/8

ACTING
6/8

QUALITY
5/8

REWATCH
4/4

CREEPS
3/4

GIMMICK
3/4

Tales from the Crypt comes out as a pleasant surprise after the lesser two entries. Some will find it even surpasses on many levels the first installment in the Amicus collection, Dr. Terror's House of Horrors. It is also arguably the most creative anthology in the franchise. It avoids relying on classic monsters to tell its horrors and it is the ultimate reason it succeeds so well.

The segments are all highly entertaining. The twists are brilliant and hard to predict. The different narratives used are unprecedented. The same can be said about set and production design. Because Tales from the Crypt takes its source material from popular EC Comic publications, the sets are high in color, contrast and show great depth and detail.

The antagonists are varied and all interesting. They bring their own world into their respective segments. Evil Santa, a genie hiding in a statuette, a revenant, Valentine's Day pranksters and a berserk dog; this anthology can seemingly make anything or anyone as amusing as scary. Tales from the Crypt offers five horror stories in which the bad guys get it worse than their victims...

Tales of Terror

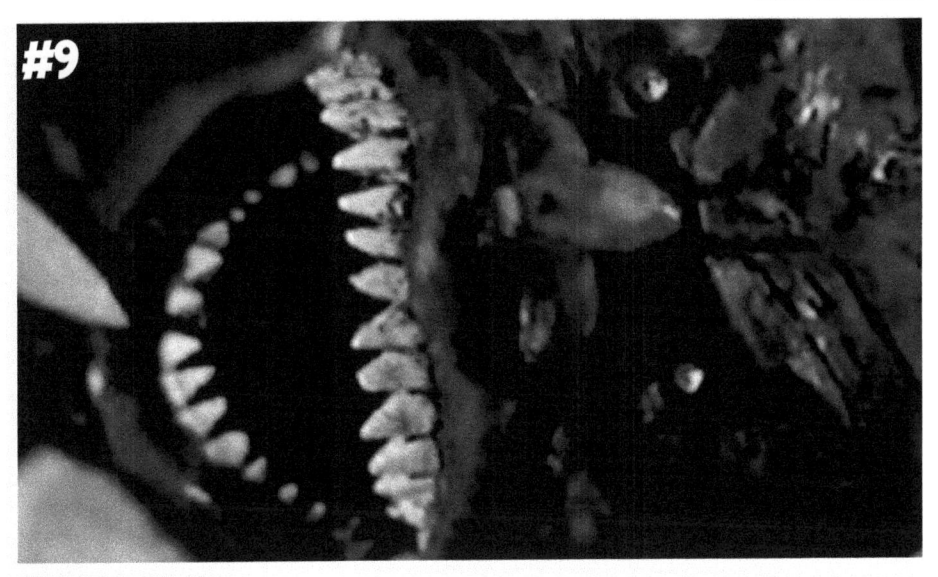

TRILOGY OF TERROR II

1996

Different people become victims of evil forces.

STARS 6/8
STORY 6/8
CREATIVITY 7/8
ACTING 6/8
QUALITY 6/8
REWATCH 4/4
CREEPS 3/4
GIMMICK 3/4

Odd human relationships are at the center of Trilogy of Terror 2, which was also the case in the original film. And then, there is the return of the Zuni doll, trademark of the original Trilogy of Terror! Fun and irony are what makes this sequel appealing and accessible. Every tale starts somewhat seriously, then descends into madness and hilarity until the twist hits.

The special effects aren't Trilogy of Terror 2's best feature. The stories aren't perfect. The first tale gets stale during its second half, for instance. The film looks good. It's creepy most of the time. It creates escalating tension and sometimes claustrophobia. All tales have an element of seclusion to them. The segments are a good combo. Interesting antagonists and subgenres are explored.

The third tale is a nice surprise. It is in fact a direct sequel to the third tale of the first Trilogy of Terror. Those who vaguely remember Trilogy of Terror might still have a vivid memory of the Zuni doll story featuring Karen Black. Many horror anthology films contain a segment about a small creature and here Trilogy of Terror keeps the tradition up. It is the best segment of the bunch.

WWW.TERROR.CA   53

Anthologies of Terror

#8

TRILOGY OF TERROR

1975

Different socially struggling individuals meet their dark fate.

STARS 6/8
STORY 6/8
CREATIVITY 7/8
ACTING 7/8
QUALITY 6/8
REWATCH 4/4
CREEPS 3/4
GIMMICK 3/4

Karen Black interprets four roles in this top tier horror anthology. She is at the center of every tale and displays a wide range of subtleties, supported by other strong actors. Trilogy of Terror evenly deals with visceral, psychological and supernatural fears, and skillfully glorifies a bunch of unlikely antagonists. Although basic, the stories are captivating and increasingly inventive.

Conflictual relationships are the main theme. In the first story, a prude teacher is seduced by her young student. The second one introduces two sisters whose reasons for hating each other is the core intrigue. Last but not least is a simple story about a cursed wooden doll trying to kill a bachelorette; incessantly chasing her down in her own apartment, something popularized by 1972's Asylum.

The film is textured to perfection, a syndrome of the high budget releases of the era, and the tales are visually homogeneous. Despite their surreal or supernatural tangents, they are all deeply rooted in the thriller subgenre, into horror comics and compartmentalized science fiction of the 50's. The end result is a short and nicely packaged compilation with surprising concepts and keen imagery.

Tales of Terror

CAMPFIRE TALES

1997

A bunch of teenagers whose car broken down tell each other scary stories around a campfire.

STARS 6/8
STORY 6/8
CREATIVITY 6/8
ACTING 7/8
QUALITY 7/8
REWATCH 4/4
CREEPS 3/4
GIMMICK 4/4

This is more than your average horror anthology film. It isn't especially big on special effects, but it is tense and scary nonetheless. The wraparound tale features likable characters, is captivating and ends nicely. If the two first stories didn't stretch for this long, another one could've easily fit in the compilation. Indeed, these one sentence bite-size gimmicks contain lots of filler...

All segments happen on a human level and all are, as the title indicates, takes on famous campfire tales, or "urban legends". They revolve around love or family. The first is about a couple on their honeymoon who run out of gas. The second tells the story of a girl who is stalked by a creep. The last story is the magnum opus. It is about a traveler who finds love unexpectedly.

All three stories are particularly well directed and are the result of solid screenplays. Each are directed by different men. They don't rely on jump scares and use genuine tension to keep us at the edge of our seats. The budget is decent. The actors are great. If you are an horror anthology film aficionado, then this should be at the top of your watch list.

WWW.TERROR.CA

Anthologies of Terror

#6

TALES FROM THE DARKSIDE: THE MOVIE

1990

A child tells a woman who wants to eat him three dark stories in order to buy time.

STARS 6/8
STORY 6/8
CREATIVITY 8/8
ACTING 7/8
QUALITY 7/8
REWATCH 4/4
CREEPS 3/4
GIMMICK 4/4

Tales from the Darkside: The Movie is based on the anthology television series Tales from the Darkside. It is a collection of three supernatural horror stories all equally entertaining and all equally frightening. Being directed by George A. Romero, this could've easily been intended as Creepshow 3, which, at some point, has been rumored but never confirmed.

Segment one tells the story of three graduates who meddle with an old enchanted sarcophagus on campus and awaken an evil mummy. Segment two is about an old man who hires a hit man to take care of a black cat that has been terrorizing him for years. The last segment is about a man who meets a gargoyle-like monster that forces him to swear he'll never tell anyone about his encounter.

The wraparound segment is shocking but oh so amusing. It is about a paperboy who was kidnapped by a cannibal woman, as we learn, and tells her stories from a book; the three segments, in order to delay supper time. Tales from the Darkside: The Movie is one of the best horror anthology films out there. It has significant production value and it is written and directed with great talent.

Tales of Terror

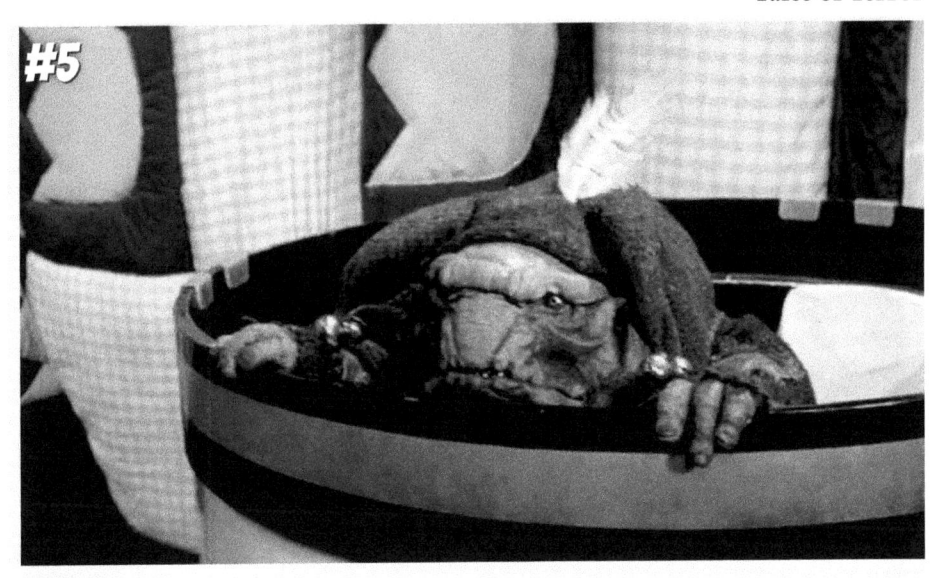

#5

CAT'S EYE

1985

A stray cat meets evil wherever it goes.

STARS 7/8
STORY 6/8
CREATIVITY 6/8
ACTING 7/8
QUALITY 7/8
REWATCH 4/4
CREEPS 3/4
GIMMICK 4/4

Cat's Eye was written by Stephen King and directed by Lewis Teague. King's wit shows every step of the way. His characters are likable but cynical caricatures. The movie is titled Cat's Eye because its three segments are unified by the short passage of a stray cat. All three tales end with an ironic or karmic conclusion and the cat carries us to the next step.

Story 1 is about a man who receives deadly incentives to quit smoking. The cure starts lightly and escalates into torture. Story 2 is the most stressful and involves a man walking on the ledge of a skyscraper. This one will mark you if you suffer from vertigo! Story 3 is about a troll attempting to suffocate a girl while she is asleep. It isn't a bad segment but it is the weakest one.

The effects that rely most on brightness, contrast and deep blacks reveal heavy flaws on high definition. Lewis Teague pulled small miracles to assemble a nearly perfect horror anthology, but he doesn't master every aspect of photography. He can coordinate actors skillfully, though. The performances are excellent. We get many familiar faces and an ideal casting.

Anthologies of Terror

#4

TRICK 'R TREAT

2007

A Halloween night turns into a blood bath for different groups of people connected to each other.

STARS 7/8
STORY 6/8
CREATIVITY 8/8
ACTING 8/8
QUALITY 8/8
REWATCH 4/4
CREEPS 3/4
GIMMICK 4/4

This is one of the best horror anthology films ever made. It is right up there with Creepshow and Trilogy of Terror. It sets itself apart from the norm by the way it intertwines 6 segments. Things happen before, during and after another, and we're never sure in which order. The script is brilliantly layered in a way to juxtapose stories seamlessly. Michael Dougherty orchestrates this like a king.

The photography is so precise and so optimized that Dougherty earns our attention from frame one. The scary parts are scary, the build-up is outstanding, the gore striking, the stories original and the twists surprising. Gore feels real and so does the rest of the effects. Trick 'r Treat's major flaw is that its tales feel incomplete despite an intention to innovate with a new kind of narrative.

Story 1 doesn't stand on its own but sets the tone nicely. Story 2 is about a man who gives a kid poisoned candy. Story 3 follows a bunch of teenagers who play a prank on a friend. Story 4 is about a special party in a remote location. Story 5 introduces a small demonic character who will teach a hermit a lesson. This is the best story in the pack. Story 6 ties the last lose ends nicely.

Tales of Terror

#3 TWILIGHT ZONE: THE MOVIE

1983

Different sets of people experiment supernatural phenomena.

STARS
7/8

STORY
7/8

CREATIVITY
8/8

ACTING
7/8

QUALITY
7/8

REWATCH
4/4

CREEPS
3/4

GIMMICK
4/4

The Twilight Zone was a popular science-fiction TV series that originally aired in the 1950's and 1960's and would mark a generation. Twilight Zone: The Movie takes four of the original tales and gives them a significant upgrade. The themes explored are racism, aging, family and mental illness. As a rule of thumb, the more we advance in the film, the better the stories get.

The first segment is very taboo. The protagonist is a racist man who suddenly becomes the martyr of every ethnicity he hates. The second story turns a handful of elders young again and makes us reflect on aging and death. It is beautiful, soothing and sad. Story 3; the most creative, has the best special effects and craziest storyline. Story 4 is terrifying and will make you fear airplanes.

Twilight Zone: The Movie is in the upper tier of anthology films. It starts with science fiction and fantasy then slowly escalates into terror. It was written and directed by the best filmmakers around and is way ahead of its time. On a technical level, this production is nearly flawless. If the two first tales don't stick with you long after you've watched this, the last two will...

WWW.TERROR.CA

Anthologies of Terror

#2

CREEPSHOW 2

1987

A storytelling specter assists a boy in plotting revenge against bullies.

STARS 8/8
STORY 6/8
CREATIVITY 8/8
ACTING 6/8
QUALITY 6/8
REWATCH 4/4
CREEPS 4/4
GIMMICK 3/4

As a novelty in a now official anthology franchise, Creepshow 2 is fully animated with a decent frame-by-frame render between its segments. The wrap-around story is amusing, looks made for kids, but culminates into something sinister, of course. The comic book element has been replaced by cartoon renditions, but this sequel feels continuous otherwise.

The tales are once again from Stephen King and George A. Romero's pens, but the directorial chair has been filled by a newcomer. Having the horror legends taking a slight step aside doesn't impact the production quality in any way. In fact, Creepshow 2 outdoes itself on many levels. The actors aren't as famous as they were in part 1, but they do a convincing job.

Part 1 had five stories and this one only three. First, we meet an avenging statue, then a hungry oil patch and, finally, an angry hobo. The three scripts are thin, so the limited amount of segment isn't justified. Because the stories are longer but not denser than those of the previous film, they burn slowly. Despite a weak last third, Creepshow 2 is one of the best released horror anthologies.

Tales of Terror

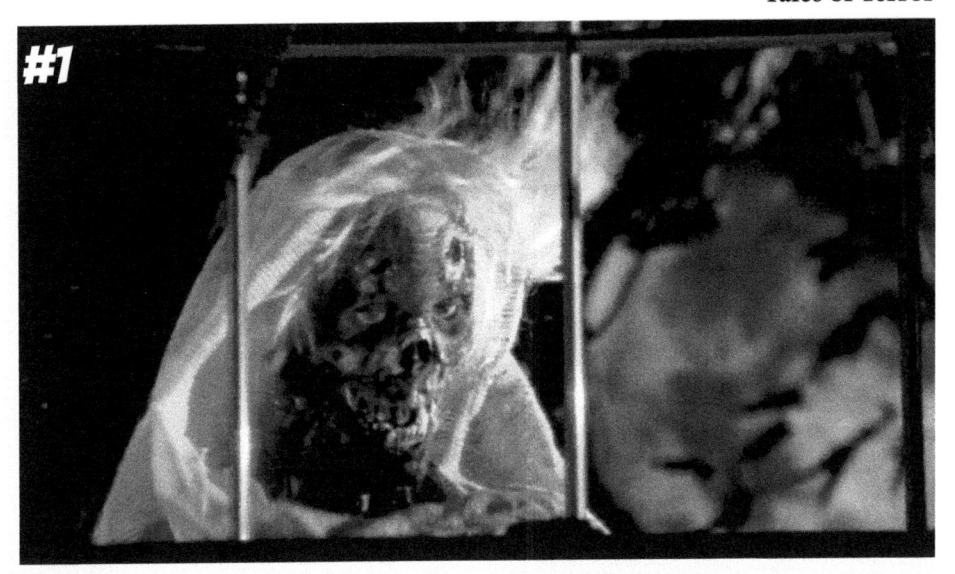

#1

CREEPSHOW

1982

A monster escapes from a horror comic book and visits a battered boy to inspire him in his vengeance scheme.

STARS
8/8
STORY
6/8
CREATIVITY
8/8
ACTING
6/8
QUALITY
6/8
REWATCH
4/4
CREEPS
4/4
GIMMICK
3/4

As if right out of an EC Comic, Creepshow uses a variety of colored lights and gobos. Still painting morphs into real footage, then back to comic world to isolate each of the 5 segments. The wrap-around story centers on the frustrations of a young boy who gets physically abused by his father, and is, in itself, a strong story featuring unique effects and surreal sociopath characters.

There's something for everyone in this anthology, namely evil ex-lovers, monsters, alien forms, plants, bugs and revenants. There's light humor and always a comical lesson to be learned; mostly through situation reversals. The acting is solid and delivered by familiar names who provide delightful caricatural performances. Both the protagonists and the antagonists make quite an impression.

The gore design and the creature costumes aren't targeting realism, but they are scary nonetheless. Based on Stephen King's writing and directed by the excellent George A. Romero, the movie is well-structured, well-paced, concise, and displays an impressive level of uniformity across its different tales. Creepshow is unarguably one of the best horror anthologies out there.

WWW.TERROR.CA   61